For information about this title or to order other books
and/or electronic media, contact the publisher:

Artistic Electronic Commerce, LLC
rick.steele@selectshops.com

ISBN: 978-0-9985194-0-1

Illustrated by Elettra Cudignotto
Cover and Interior design: 1106 Design

Printed in the United States of America

Dedication

*This book wouldn't be possible
if not for the quick-thinking actions
of a tiny, strawberry blonde, freckled chipmunk :)
You've battled through a lot kiddo.
You are one of my Four Heroes in life!*

*To all the parents out there with kids that
seem to lose something all the time . . . enjoy!*

"I can't find my blanket!" Isabella cried,
to her sister Elise, who grumpily replied,

"I don't know where it is, and I'm reading a book.
Get out of my room, and ask Ethan to look."

Isabella went to find
her busy little brother
but he said,
"I don't know.
Did you ask mother?"

At bedtime,
Isabella's blanket was still lost.
She tried to fall asleep
but only turned and tossed.

7

Elise finished her book, brushed her teeth, and jumped in bed,
and saw her Bedtime Bunny, lying near her head.

Then she remembered how her sister couldn't find
her favorite pink blanket and how she'd been unkind.

So she slipped from the covers,
without a single peep,
And gave her bunny to Izzie
to help her sister sleep.

"Thank you, Elise,"
Isabella tearfully said.
The two sisters hugged before
Elise went back to bed.

But on the way to her room, brother Ethan flew by
on his skateboard – in the hall! – oh me, oh my!

"Don't skateboard in the house – you'll get in trouble, mister!"
But Ethan just laughed and rolled past his sister.

Until , , , he fell down with a big, loud boom
and caused Isabella to flee from her room.

The children were making quite a commotion
until they heard father's voice, loud with emotion

"To bed! To bed!" was all he could say,
so the lights went out at the family's house that day.

And all was quiet . . . the children finally slept.
Not one peep was heard until something crept . . .

It was Bedtime Bunny, who slid down to crawl,
and find Ethan's skateboard, still in the hall.

"Wake up, Skateboard!
We have to go find
Isabella's blanket –
we can't waste any time!"

Skateboard was tired,
after all the hard play
but bowed to Bunny's need
for him to lead the way.

Carefully they traveled
down the steep stairs
as quietly as possible –
the family unaware.

"Look under the couch!"
Bedtime Bunny commanded.
So Skateboard slipped under
until he was stranded!

"I'm stuck! I'm stuck!"
he shouted out to Bunny,
"But I did find some pocket change —
quite a sum of money."

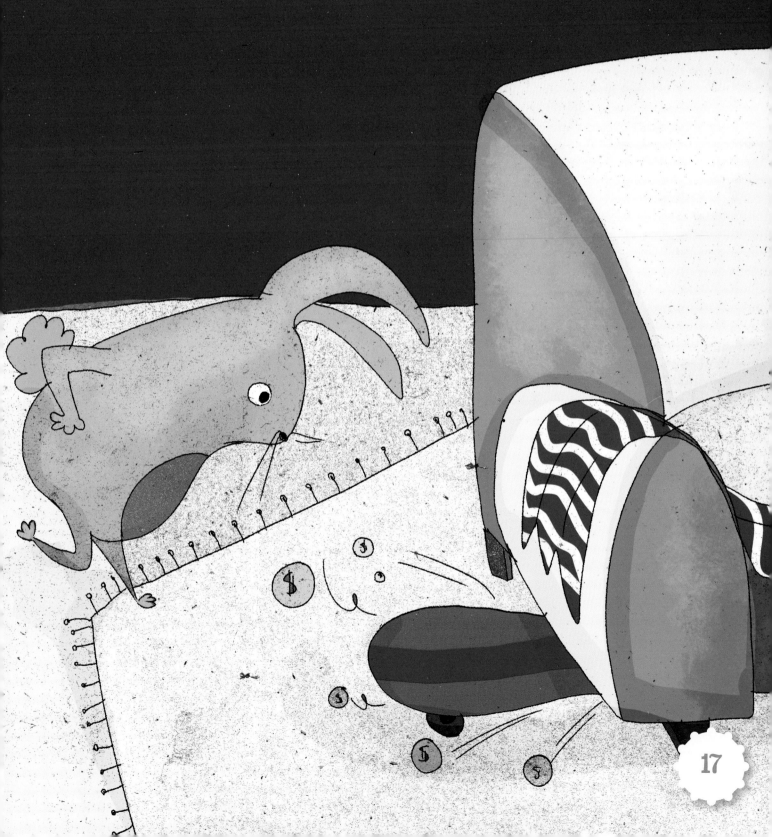

Bedtime Bunny pulled.
Bedtime Bunny pushed.
But Skateboard was lodged
and actually quite "smooshed."

What were they going to do?
Bunny didn't know.
He hopped back and forth
until he saw a glow.

Climbing on the couch,
he saw that it was Bike!
Sitting on the lawn,
sleeping in the night.

He hopped to the window
and tapped on the glass
until Bike woke up
and rode across the grass.

19

Bunny tried to tell him that Skateboard was stuck,
but Bike couldn't hear him, so they were out of luck.

Besides, it wasn't possible to get Bike in the house
when all the doors were locked and it was quiet as a mouse.

Skateboard grew sleepy in that warm, cozy place
and he began to snore — much to his disgrace.

"Wake up!" Bunny cried. "Don't you understand?
We have to find Pink Blanket, and I think I have a plan!"

Bunny hopped through the kitchen
and to the back door
where Tyson the puppy
slept on the floor.

"Hey, there, big boy,"
Bunny said to the pup,
"Skateboard needs your help,
so you need to get up!"

Tyson didn't understand
what was going on
but he wanted to help,
so he followed along.

Bunny told Tyson
to grab with his teeth
the part of Skateboard
sticking out from underneath.

"Pull! Pull! Pull!"
Bunny said a whole bunch,
so the dog bit down on poor
Skateboard with a crunch!

"Ouch!" Skateboard cried, but Tyson kept on biting
until he was free; it was all so exciting.

"Now to find Blanket!" Bunny made the decision.
But Tyson went back to bed, bored with the mission.

So into the family room
Skateboard flew
with Bunny's clear warning,
"We're coming through!"

The other toys awoke
with the rattle and clatter
and gathered 'round, asking,
"What on earth is the matter?"

"Pink Blanket is lost,"
Bunny said, quite direct.
And all the toys began
to search and inspect.

Under the desk,
under each chair,
in the children's toy bin –
just everywhere . . .

Around the corner sat a laundry basket
and there she was . . . under a jacket!

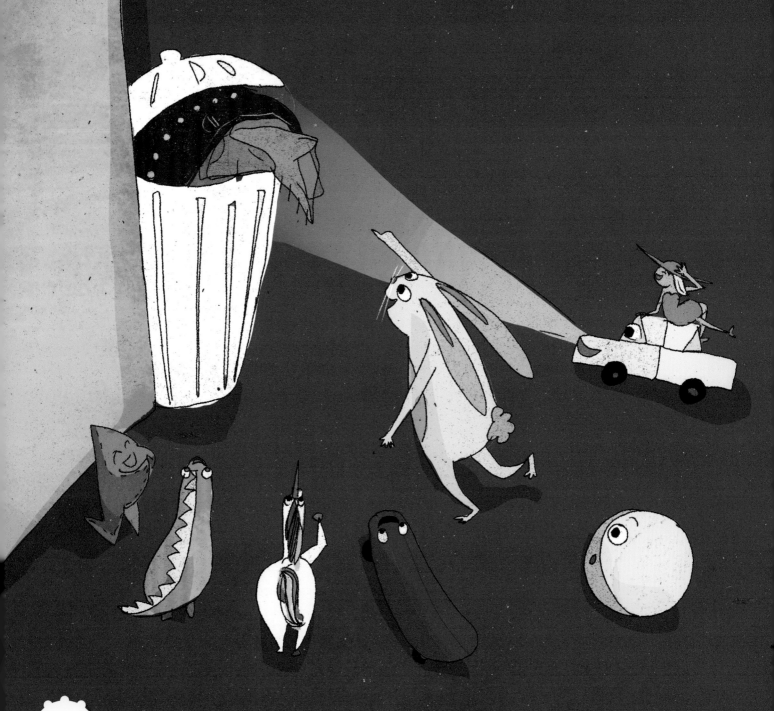

30

"She's found! She's found!" everyone cried.
Pink Blanket was safe but a bit surprised.

"What's all the fuss?"
she asked, looking 'round.
Bunny explained that
she'd finally been found.

"Oh," she said,
"I didn't know I was lost.
I was just waiting in the basket
to be washed."

They all laughed and laughed
and laughed some more!
(until they woke poor Tyson —
in the middle of a snore).

"Let's get back to bed," Bunny decided,
"before the sun comes up and all of us are sighted."

So Skateboard and Bunny crept back up the stairs
to put Blanket next to Isabella with care.

Next, Bunny climbed up
to snuggle with **Elise**
and fell peacefully asleep,
quickly, with ease.

Skateboard parked himself
once again
on the floor in the hallway,
where he'd formerly been.

And as the sun rose on the Steele household,
the children awoke , , , and, lo and behold!

Isabella went running with shouts of delight,
"Someone found my blanket during the night!"

39

"It wasn't me," said Elise with a yawn.

"It wasn't me," echoed Ethan at dawn.

"Then, who was it?
Who could it be?"

But they never would solve
this great mystery . . .

THE END

About the Author

Rick H. Steele is an award-winning speaker, adventure athlete, author, and serial entrepreneur. He's also a "cereal" entrepreneur because he loves a good bowl of Cap'n Crunch® the night before a big race. Rick is a dedicated husband, father, and friend.

About the Illustrator

Elettra Cudignotto is a freelance illustrator from Vicenza, Italy. Born in 1990, Elettra has spent her entire life drawing for herself and friends. With a Masters Degree in Economics and Management of Arts and a Degree in Visual Arts, she made the decision to follow her heart and draw all day long as a freelancer! Her work is done in a rough, digital format because of her love for textures, brushes, vivid colors and random lines.